Dad a
Grizzly Bear

Written by Jill Eggleton
Illustrated by Raymond McGrath

Dad and the kids
were going camping
in the mountains.

They saw a sign
on a tree.

"Grizzly bears live here,"
said Dad.
"This is their home."

When Dad and the kids
got up the mountain,
they put up the tent.
"Look," said the kids.
"There are bear tracks."

4

"I'll put the food in the tree,"
said Dad.
"They won't bother us then."

But in the night
something went bump
on the tent.
Everyone woke up.
"Keep still," said Dad.
"I think it's a bear."

The bear pushed the tent.
It pushed so hard,
the tent came down.
"Keep **very** still," said Dad.

The bear went
sniff, sniff, sniff.
It went **sniff, sniff, sniff**
around the tent.

It went sniff, sniff, sniff
around the tree.
But the bear could not get
any food, so it went away.

9

Dad and the kids came
out from under the tent.
"We're not sleeping here
anymore," said the kids.

10

"We'll put the tent in the tree.
We can sleep up there.
Grizzly bears
don't climb trees."

So Dad and the kids
put the tent in the tree.
"This is a cool bed,"
said the kids.
"It's like a big swing."

12

The kids went to sleep,
but they went
wiggle, wiggle
and the bed went
wobble, wobble.

Dad couldn't sleep.
He got off the tent and
sat on a branch.
But the birds went
squawk, squawk.

"It's OK," said Dad.
"It's just for **one** night!"

14

A Story Sequence

Guide Notes

Title: Dad and the Grizzly Bear
Stage: Early (4) – Green

Genre: Fiction
Approach: Guided Reading
Processes: Thinking Critically, Exploring Language, Processing Information
Written and Visual Focus: Story Sequence, Speech Bubble
Word Count: 240

THINKING CRITICALLY
(sample questions)
- What do you think this story could be about? Look at the title and discuss.
- Look at the cover. How do you think Dad feels about the bear?
- Look at pages 2 and 3. Why do you think the sign warns people not to keep food in their tents?
- Look at pages 4 and 5. Where else do you think Dad could put the food?
- Look at pages 6 and 7. How do you think Dad and the kids felt?
- Look at pages 8 and 9. What do you think Dad and the children could do to scare the bear away?
- Look at pages 12 and 13. Why do you think Dad is worried about the bed wiggling and wobbling?

EXPLORING LANGUAGE

Terminology
Title, cover, illustrations, author, illustrator

Vocabulary
Interest words: grizzly bear, camping, mountains, bother, branch
High-frequency words: something, everyone, think, any
Positional words: up, in, on, down, under
Compound words: something, everyone, anymore

Print Conventions
Capital letter for sentence beginnings and names (**D**ad), periods, commas, exclamation mark, quotation marks